SURPRISE BILLIONAIRE

A Billionaire Rogue Novella

MAGGIE TWAIN

CONTENTS

No ordinary hobo!

Having grown up on the streets, Thor's business model is simple; dress like a hobo and after being refused service, buy the company and fire everyone involved. After entering one fine dining restaurant, however, he's presented with just one problem ... the waitress is actually being nice. Oh, and she just happens to be the hottest girl he's ever seen.

Can Thor win her over, given he looks homeless and smells like manure?

Bullied by her supervisor, Angel's been told to throw out the poor homeless guy or else be fired. But she refuses to be mean to a guy down on his luck. Besides, for a hobo, he's kinda cute.

Maybe there's more to this guy than meets the eye?

If you like seductive billionaire rogues and sweet young women in their primes then you'll be enchanted by Surprise Billionaire, the latest novella by Maggie Twain.

Mature young adult / new adult: sexual content and language. For readers 17 and older.

For fans of Alexa Riley, Lucy Darling, Mink and Ella Goode.

CHAPTER ONE

Angel

I'd been warned about Mr. Carrington.

Not that I needed warning because the whole town has always known about him, about what he's like and how he likes things done.

"We're the most upmarket restaurant for miles, which is why I require all my staff to be a certain *way*," he says the word with an odd emphasis, like there's a high level of expectation placed upon the restaurant staff.

Luckily, I've had a life of forewarning but decide to ask for clarification anyway, and because I know it's what he's expecting. "How do you mean?"

He leans back in his seat and crosses one leg over the other whilst never taking his shrewd, bespectacled eyes from me. He's not creepy in the slightest, in fact, judging by his mannerisms, I question whether he likes women at all, but he still gives me an uneasy feeling, regardless, and I get the impression that this is a man who drives his employees like a plantation owner does his slaves. "You must look absolutely impeccable at all times. I need my staff to be beyond professional. There's a reason our online reviews are always so glowing. It's because our staff are the best."

I hum in a way that attempts to reassure him, even though I'm slowly beginning to lose hope he'll want to employ a girl like me.

Mr. Carrington already knows this would be my first job, naive and straight out of high school as I am, so again I can only wonder what he means by *the best* considering I have absolutely no experience. Truth is, right about now I ought to have been going to college, culinary school to be precise, but I had to abandon those plans when dad died and left my mom with twelve-year-old triplet girls and a mountain of debt. Oh, and me as well, which is why I now have to take on the responsibility of breadwinner at the tender age of eighteen. So I won't get to study to become a chef but what I do get is the next best thing, kind of, I get to carry food to and from the kitchen - I don't know whether to laugh or cry - and that's *if* I even get this waitressing job, which is unlikely.

He surveys my hair, which today is tied back neatly into a bun, about as professional as I've ever seen myself look. He motions with a hand and for a nervous moment I wonder what he's gesturing at, but then he coughs and I give him a funny look.

"Yes?"

He quietly sighs because clearly, there's something I'm not quite getting. "Please stand, Angel, and give me a spin, please."

Ah, now I'm getting the idea, by "impeccable," he means the way we look.

Although I've never considered myself *impeccable* in the

looks department, or barely even average for that matter, Mr. Carrington had obviously seen the photograph I sent with my application so I can safely assume that in his opinion, I already meet the standard for working at his restaurant. At least, that's what I tell myself.

But I really, really need this job so there's nothing else for it, I brace myself to be scrutinized like a piece of meat and stand before making a nervous half turn and then go back the other way. Yep, definitely gay, I decide, as his observation seems all business, more like how a fashion buyer might eye a set of fabrics than a new girl in the prime of her life. Or maybe I'm just not to his taste, which suits me fine. At least the man's good enough not to overtly leer at my ass, or even give an appreciative hum, and again I fear I'll be turned down for the job.

I'm really nervous.

Finally, he nods. "The job pays minimum wage but your tips will bring you out above that, so it is what you make of it. Be an impeccable waitress and you'll not go hungry. I'll email you our guidelines and rules, along with your contract."

I crush my lips together to suppress the screams of delight that are trying to escape me, because it looks like I'm hired. "Yes, um, thank you so..."

"Collect your uniform on the way downstairs. You can start tomorrow. Alma will show you the ropes." He waves me out the room so I leave before he can change his mind.

And with that, I have my first ever job, and although it's not what I might have dreamed about, it's a start and I'm on my way. Chef school will have to wait until my sisters are grown up. Until then, maybe I can pry on the chefs here.

That night, I'm almost too excited to sleep, but I manage a few hours and rise early so I have plenty of time to get ready and to ensure I look perfect. "Impeccable, damn it." I pay particular attention to my hair and makeup before spending considerable effort pressing all the creases out of my uniform. By the time I'm ready to leave, I think I scrub up pretty well. My mom wishes me luck, I hug and kiss Kelly, Holly and Tilly, and then I'm out the door to catch the bus.

I arrive in the staffroom early to meet my new colleagues but am dismayed to find there's barely a happy face in the building, and that includes my friend Clare.

"Hey babe, I'm so glad to have a friendly face with me at this dump," she sighs and gestures about to the ten or twelve other employees wearing a range of uniforms and all sitting with glum expressions. "As you can see, we're in need of some life around this dive."

"Hey, shush, these people have ears, you know." I give a small, nervous wave to at least try to appear friendly and one or two people murmur something back out of politeness. But whoa, the place truly is miserable, and I'm about to ask why when she prods me in the ribs with an elbow.

"Oh, relax," with the flap of a dainty hand, she dismisses her earlier words, "if I wasn't around to banter, there'd be nobody else and then we might as well be working at a funeral parlor." She shakes her head at a young waiter who's staring at the clock with a look of what can only be described as pain. "Sometimes, it's easy to get the two mixed up."

"Clare..." I almost grab ahold of her shoulders to give her a shake but then remember where I am.

"Hey, it's cool," she nudges me, "as long as you're at least pretending to be happy around the customers then nobody cares what we say or do back here during the seven minutes a day we get to ourselves."

I tut and want to tell her to stop denigrating my new place of employment. I know she's joking, I hope, but she's killing the buzz I've felt since yesterday and besides, I have absolutely no reason to be anything but perfectly happy. I'm a happy person. Nobody's forcing anyone to work here, other than the fact it's a small town and Carrington's happens to be one of the largest employers around which, I suppose, might be good enough reason we're all stuck. Oh, shucks, maybe Clare does have a point. I'm keen to change the subject. "Which one's Alma?" I glance around at the glum faces. "She's supposed to be showing me the ropes."

Clare bristles at the mention of the name but before she can answer, the door opens and an older woman clips inside.

She looks to be in her early fifties with a pinched face and brown hair tied up into the tightest bun I've ever seen, so tight, in fact, that it almost appears to be pulling back the skin on her face. It's her eyes though that tell the story, like she's seen it all and nothing can get passed her. Most ominously of all, however, is that the room fell into complete silence the moment she stepped inside. At least one girl turns away.

I find myself frozen and unable to look away from the woman, who I have a suspicion must be Alma, and then she finds me, standing in the center of the room and feeling suddenly very exposed.

"Hi," I manage to utter whilst making another tiny

wave that doubtless I'm soon gonna be known for around here.

Her mouth tightens as she gives me the full-on appraisal, up and down, repeat, already far more severe than Mr. Carrington. She fixes on my blouse, freshly pressed, I might add, and her nose scrunches.

Clare leans close to my ear. "That would be Alma, my dear." As if I didn't already know. "She a bitch."

"You must be the new girl," she states matter of fact. I guess it's kind of obvious. I give another pathetic little wave and tilt my hip but her eyes are fixed on my blouse again. "Your uniform's not pressed." I want to object because my uniform's immaculate, but being the sudden center of attention, I find myself unable to say anything. Her eyes never leave me and I can feel myself wilting under her gaze. "If you bothered to read your contract then you'd know that's a disciplinary offense."

I take a sudden sharp intake of air, she's being so mean to chastise me on my first day, and in front of everyone too. It's just not the decent way of doing things. But what can I do? Nothing, is what. And I *did* read the contract. Twice, in fact.

She gives me a final look as the skin between her eyes bunches, which threatens to unsettle her hair, and then she taps her watch and cries out to everyone, "right, it's time. Get to your posts."

Coffees are quickly drained and Clare tugs me closer. "And that, Angel, is why we're all so fucking miserable."

I get the impression I really need to remain on Alma's good side.

How hard can it be?

I spend the first hour simply tailing Clare, watching

and observing as she takes orders for coffee, pancakes, croissants, fresh orange juice, eggs Benedict and even the occasional bowl of oatmeal. Yuck. Whenever I get the chance, I hover in the kitchen and watch with fascination the attention to detail as the chefs work magic with ingredients, turning them into dishes that resemble works of art. It's what I should be doing, damnit. I then have to carry them out to the customers and in less than an hour, my belly's rumbling terribly. I grab two breakfasts from the counter whilst muttering "table twelve," so I don't forget where they're going, turn around and just narrowly miss clobbering into Alma as she's coming up from behind.

"Hey, watch it, you nearly caused an accident." She's flashing her teeth and I feel my eyes widen of their own accord.

"Oh, gosh, I'm so sorry, I'll be more careful in future."

"Yes, you'd better." Her lips fall back down as she takes the moment to again survey my appearance, and I question whether I detect a sniff. "Your uniform's not pressed."

For a moment, I can only wonder if she's mad, but I'm too cowed to mention she already told me that. "Yes, I'm, um, sorry, I'll do better tomorrow," I say instead and can feel the perspiration dripping down my back. Kitchens are hot, which is something I'll have to get used to.

Her arms fold and I find my eyes darting to the plates I'm holding, two eggs royale, which will soon go cold in contravention of Carrington's standards. She continues to bar my exit. "In future, always make sure you press your uniform. *Every* morning. At Carrington's, we're impeccable." There's that word again.

But this has to be a power trip. She must be able to see

my uniform's pressed but I have no doubt she'd find fault with something no matter what. No, better just take the abuse, let her see she has me cowed and with a bit of luck, when she knows I'm a hard worker, then I'll be able to win her over. Hopefully. Let's face it, I have no other plan. There's certainly no point arguing with her, especially when she's my direct supervisor. Finally, she steps aside and I continue on my way whilst I can feel her stare burning into my back.

I catch Clare's eye just as she's untying her apron strings. "Hey, it's my break so it looks like for the next twenty minutes, you've got the place to yourself," she gives me a reassuring rub of the arm to let me know I can do this and then she disappears into the staffroom as she taps at her cell screen.

"Oh, gosh, so this is really it." Sink or swim, sink or swim. *Stay cool, Angel, now's your chance to prove yourself to Alma.*

A party of four enter the establishment and gaze about at the high ceilings and chandeliers. I'm nervous as I approach but I show them to a table and present them all with menus. Another group is already waiting to be seated and I do the same for them before returning to the first party and taking their orders. My arms are shaking but I'm slowly beginning to get the idea I can really do this.

I will always remember the first order I took as a waitress, which was for five pancakes stacked on top of each other, all drizzled with syrup and sprinkled with cinnamon. The coffee is a rare Ethiopian blend and I can't resist breathing in the delectable aroma as I'm taking it over. I mention how they're my first customers as a waitress and they're thrilled for me and when it comes time to settle the bill, they give me a huge tip, as does the second group.

By the time morning is over, I'm thrilled to have made considerably more money in tips than I have from my actual wage. I thrust all the money into the tip jar and Janice and Karl both beam wide smiles and suddenly people don't seem so miserable as they did before. Clare had already told me the tips are shared amongst everyone at the end of the day so if one waitress is having a particularly good shift, we all benefit.

"Goodbye student loans," Ben, the guy who'd earlier been staring at the clock, dreading the start of his shift, gives me a high five. What a turnaround.

I dismiss all the praise with a flap of a hand, even though I'm struggling to hide my grin. It's so nice to receive such praise after only having been here a few hours.

By the time my shift is over, I've made considerably more tips, and Clare mumbles something about it being a restaurant record, at least for the time she's been working at Carrington's, and I'm so happy because there are things I really need to do with that money, like pay my mom's rent, because that's one thing she always struggles with, despite the fact she works so hard. There's also the small matter of the triplets, who're all growing so fast out of their clothes. Maybe soon I'll be able to buy them some books for school.

When it comes time to divvying up the money, Alma takes control, which is hardly a surprise, I guess she is the boss.

"Here you are, Janice, Karl, Ben, Clare," she hands an envelope to each in turn and I'm next in line. "Not you,

Angel," she says, showing me her palm, "you contravened the restaurant rules with a crumpled uniform, so as per regulations there will be no tips for you today, but take it as a learning curve and endeavor to do better tomorrow."

Clare's mouth plunges open and I think I hear her muttering something about Alma being a bitch. Ben stares at the wad of notes he's just plucked from his envelope.

"What?" I can feel myself shaking and turning red. "The regulations say no such thing and I ... I was reading my contract only last night."

She folds her arms and looks at me from down the length of her nose. "Well, you obviously didn't read the *new* regulations, did you?"

I hiss, "what new regulations?"

She points to the noticeboard and grins in triumph. "The ones I added this morning."

"Oh," I nod and have to dig deep to hold back the tears. So this is why everybody hates Alma.

I think I understand things now.

CHAPTER TWO

Thor

I wait until I'm certain that at least two employees are watching from inside the showroom before making my move. Truth is, you'd have to be blind to miss me, considering I arrived in a piece of shit Hillman Imp still in its original rust from the seventies, which I took the liberty of parking beside an Aston Martin Vanquish, a car that costs almost three hundred grand. I should know, I own one.

A suave guy in a suit stirs from behind the large pane of shatterproof glass and continues to watch me, hands on hips. Shortly after, he's joined by a woman, who looks equally all business.

"Now, now, now," I hide the smirk but cannot suppress the surging adrenaline as I open the door and have to stoop considerably to exit the hunk of tin that's blighting the yard. I close the door but because the hinge is broken it merely clatters against the shitty steel and won't set into its frame. In full view of my two onlookers, I spend the next minute tying the door closed with string. There's no rear driver's side window, so looping the cord around the frame is easy enough.

The door holds, not that anyone would want to steal such a piece of crap anyway, but I think I've made my point to the watching staff. For sure, it looks out of place surrounded by forty Ferraris, Porsches, Lamborghinis and even a McLaren. I particularly like the look of the 570S Spider and make a mental note to buy one at some point.

I set off for the entrance and the enormous glass frontage reveals that the damned piece of shit I arrived in is rolling backwards in the direction of a particularly tasty looking Bugatti Chiron. Quite honestly, I can do without the paperwork, so I run and shove my fingers through the crack in the window, thrust it down and stretch for the handbrake.

I concede there's very little chance they didn't notice that.

But, disaster averted, I finally make for the entrance and, squeezing between a Bentley and a Rolls Royce, I see the man with his hands in his hair. They lower and now he pinches at the skin atop his nose when he realizes that yes, I truly am about to enter the business. I pause to take a breath, scratch at the fake shaggy beard I'm wearing and pretend to flick away something I find living inside it. It's a cold day and I clap my gloved hands together for warmth. When I reach the door, it says pull, so I push and spend the next few seconds shaking the door in a forlorn effort to enter. When I figure I'm meant to pull, the door's exceptionally heavy for this supposed semi-starved homeless man and it does not escape my attention that neither of the watching staff bothers to help, maybe open the door, offer their assistance, say hello. Eventually, the woman, blonde, tidy, clearly inconvenienced, struts over out of pity and opens it for me, or maybe I'm scaring away the real customers and she wants me gone and out of the way as quickly as possible.

"Good morning," I rasp and her eyes instinctively roam over my clothes, the major component being the overcoat that an hour earlier, I bought off a homeless guy for $1000. It reeks of alcohol and so far, I've been too afraid to check the pockets.

Now that I've made it inside, the man's quick to head straight for me, cutting off my gaze of the vehicles spread out across the sparkling tiles. "Yes?" He asks in a tone that suggests I'm a piece of shit he just stepped on. "May I help you?" He's older than the girl and looks like he knows how to sell expensive cars, he has that very smooth look to him, and I'm guessing he's the manager.

I try not to laugh inside, which I always find is the hardest part about doing this, and I take another step inside, puckering my lips in appreciation at all the flashy cars he's half blocking from my view. The place smells so good, but then, I'm wearing an overcoat that has probably never been washed. The man's wearing a name tag that says 'Piers' and his eyes drift down towards my feet, more specifically the farmer's boots I'm wearing, still caked in manure after my trip through the cattle field. Somehow, I can't picture Piers with a mop, cleaning the mess after I leave. The boots themselves I've owned for a long time, since way before I had any money at all, and I still find them comfortable, even if they look like they should have long ago been consigned to the trash. I keep them as a reminder of where I've come from.

I exhale and open out my arms to encompass the

vehicles inside the showroom. "I was hoping you wouldn't mind showing me your latest models, perhaps with a view to taking something out for a test." I gesture absentmindedly to my rear, to where there's a hunk of tin being held together by string. "I can use this as part exchange if that would sweeten the deal?" Again, I have to bite my tongue to stop myself from bursting into hysterics.

How I love being a billionaire, the joy I feel in these moments is worth so much more than the cars, the yachts, the penthouses, the women even. It's all in how they feel superior, that in moments like these I can see into their souls, the way they treat society's most unfortunate people, all the while I'm the only one who knows that their feeling of being better, their smiles, will soon be wiped clean off their faces.

There's another sales lady who's trying to make herself look busy at the other end of the showroom, whilst the woman who opened the door for me is waiting around, though I'm getting the impression that's because she wants to see where this is going, almost like she's taking some amusement from her manager having to deal with what they all think is a penniless hobo who's probably high on meth.

Piers again bars my path, sniffs, and coughs into a closed fist. "I'm sorry sir but I'm afraid these vehicles are somewhat out of your price range, but thank you for stopping by." At this point the girl snorts.

But this is how poor people are treated all the time, I remember those days, indeed, I will never forget them.

"Oh, I understand, sir." I make a sad face, shuffle about on my feet and clap my hands together for warmth. "In that case, I'll leave you to your business." I make a half turn but check myself.

Piers makes a show of checking his watch. "Yes?"

I sigh and lick my lips. "I don't want to be an inconvenience, but is there any chance I might perhaps have a drink from your coffee machine? It was a cold night, only three of my doors have windows and I'm thirsty."

The man sighs in a way that's meant to make me know I'm a nuisance and he then scrutinizes my face, the wig I bought from the Squatters movie set, the stick-on beard that's itching for real, at the dirt I smeared over my face before arriving, and he sniffs again at the air around me. "I'm afraid, sir, that our coffee machine is out of order and besides, our facilities are for paying customers only. I hope you understand." He nods in finality.

I nod sadly back and as usual, I find that the most difficult part of doing this is stopping myself from tearing off my disguise and flashing the Royal Gold credit card with its twenty-five thousand dollar annual fee I have inside my wallet before telling him he's just made the biggest mistake of his life. Instead, I take quiet satisfaction in the knowledge that the next time we meet, my friend Piers will be acting somewhat differently towards me.

I leave, giddy with excitement, and head for my rented penthouse apartment in the city. I throw off the wig, beard and all the dirty clothes before jumping in the shower. I take my time dressing in my usual style, the tailored suit I bought on London's Savile Row, the Italian leather shoes, I slip on my gold Rolex, cufflinks and bracelet. When I'm done, I look like a million dollars, and take a moment at the mirror to straighten my necktie, which alone is worth more than most of the cars in the place I've just left. I spray on some Clive Christian No. 1 and am about ready to go when my cell vibrates.

It's a message from my sister. *'Thor, you're doing it again, aren't you. You're such a jerk. Aren't you tired of putting the world to rights?'*

I respond with, *'you know I can't stop.'*

My cell rings. "Shit." I answer, "Sissy."

"Don't you sissy me, jerk, and don't think I don't know exactly what you've been doing."

I shrug, "what have I been doing?"

She breathes hard down the line. *"You bought my favorite bakery in town, is what you've been doing."*

My mouth curls slyly at the memory. "The pastry chef wouldn't let me take from the sampling tray, so I took his job instead."

"Listen, you complete jackass, you took everyone's job, including Milly's. She's worked there for twenty-five years. What's she supposed to do now?"

"I like to bring in my own people, you know this, and besides, it was danish he wouldn't let me sample. You know how much I love danish."

"Fuck your danishes and you were refused because you smell like you've been living in the gutter. What did you expect him to do, allow you to contaminate the whole tray of samples? You're not the only one who likes danishes, you know."

I breathe hard down the line, I'm getting annoyed now. "You know I don't stand for people being unkind to the homeless. Sissy, you must have a short memory. Just because now you live in a mansion doesn't mean you have to forget what it used to be like for us."

She's silent for a while. *"I haven't forgotten. And you're still a jerk."*

"I always will be."

I can sense her shaking her head over the distance. The long silence usually means she's about to change subject to the usual. *"Don't you think it's about time you found a good woman and settled down? Maybe that would focus your mind and besides, my children want cousins."*

I squeeze the cell and my knuckles turn white. "I have more important things than finding a woman and besides, they never seem to like me."

It's hard for her not to laugh at that. *"That's because you spend half your life looking like you sleep in a dumpster. What do you expect? Damn it, Thor, when you scrub up you could be on the cover of Men's Health magazine. You're so frustrating."*

"Father would be proud," or so I assumed, I never knew him but it's a private joke between the two of us.

"Ugh, men, I'm so glad my husband is nothing like you." There's another pause and again, I know what's coming. *"Thor, you know how much Kristina likes you..."* Kristina's her full-time life coach and new best friend, which basically means that she's an employed shadow whose job is to constantly blow smoke up my sister's ass. Maybe I pay Sissy too much for the work she does for me.

I bristle, we've had this conversation so many times. "This again?"

"Well, she does."

"Hmm, I seem to recall she wasn't all that impressed back when I was struggling with my first company, working nineteen-hour days. What changed?" I stroke my beard, it's a tough one.

"Thor, of course the money's not a complete turn-off, but I promise, it's you she likes."

"Uh-huh, right," that sure wasn't the impression I got back when I asked her out when I was outfitting my first bar. No, it's too late for Kristina, I've already seen inside her soul. "I'm sorry, Sissy."

"Ugh, I will wear you down yet, jerk."

"You still love me, right?"

"Jackass, and if my favorite red velvet cupcakes don't taste exactly the same as they have since I was a child, I swear I'll never speak to you again."

"I'm sure you'll live."

"Jackass."

"I love you too." I end the call. Now, where was I...

I take the long ride down the elevator to the underground parking lot and breeze over to where my Ferrari's waiting. I sink into the soft leather and feel the power as the engine roars to life, that same power I now feel coursing through my veins, that same power I'm about to wield to devastating effect. It's the power of money. Money is power. At least that's what people believe and for so long as people continue believing, it will continue to be true.

In less than an hour after leaving the showroom, I'm rolling up a different man and for the thousandth time, I'm about to learn just how much difference money makes to how you're treated. I park the Ferrari right beside the large glass display pane and spring out before striding confidently for the entrance.

Piers is already rushing to assist with the door. "Good morning, sir," he says without the slightest hint of realization that we're already acquainted, kind of, "welcome to Astor's. If you require any assistance then please don't hesitate to ask."

For some reason, I'm almost pissed when usually I'm buzzing about now. Perhaps it was the conversation with my sister. "Oh, I'm sure we'll be having words very soon indeed, you can trust me on that."

"Excellent," he nods and smiles, "in the meantime, can I get you anything? A glass of water, a cup of coffee, perhaps?"

I was in the process of stepping further inside but that checked me. "You mean, your coffee machine's working?" I ask with a squint.

He doesn't so much as flinch, "of course. Clara?" he calls across the length of the showroom, "one coffee for the gentleman, if you'd be so kind."

A minute later, the girl who'd earlier snorted at me and who'd proven equally unhelpful brings over a cup on a saucer. I accept it with good grace and it's not lost on me the way she checks me out in my expertly tailored suit. She has no clue either.

I inhale the aroma, it's definitely not cheap vending machine crap. "A Central American blend?" I take a sip. "Costa Rica, maybe Panama?"

Clara puckers her lips in appreciation. "Panama would be correct." She's about to say something else but I turn away before she can speak and begin stepping across the tiles, admiring the beautiful craftsmanship of their overpriced wares whilst they follow closely behind like a pair of puppies.

Piers' voice comes from near my ass. "Would you like to see the latest Ferrari, or how about our newest Porsche model?"

Suddenly, I turn on a very expensive Italian heel. "You know something, what I'd really like is to meet the owner of this fine purveyor of luxury cars."

Now, this is the point where the reactions often differ. Mostly, they're happy to oblige because hey, I just arrived in a Ferrari and like I always say, people are very good to you when they know you have money. Very often, they'll make excuses and attempt to deal with you themselves, especially when commission's involved. Occasionally, your demand is refused outright or they might even lie, saying the manager's not present and you should deal with them instead. On this occasion, Piers merely blinks away his surprise but is soon on the phone to the owner, who I'm told needs thirty minutes to arrive from across town.

I stand around, sipping coffee, admiring the cars and being admired by Clara. Eventually, a very smart looking Range Rover SUV pulls into the lot and then an older man, perhaps seventy years of age with white hair, gets out and steps into the showroom. Earlier, I'd overheard Piers telling him there's a customer who requires particular treatment and he'd like it from the owner, which is not unusual when dealing with high-end items, in fact it's often how I like to roll.

"Hello, sir, I'm Mr. Astor," he holds out his hand and I can tell immediately he's an old-style gentleman, "how might I be of assistance?"

I take his hand and glance airily toward the far side of the showroom before suggesting that we take a meeting in his office. His eyes widen in slight surprise as Piers' eyebrows furrow on his head, as well they might, but he leads the way and then he's gesturing for me to take a seat in a comfortable Chesterfield style couch in an office decorated in a way that betrays the man's age. I'll soon get my people in to give it a modern touch.

He sits behind the big desk and opens out his palms. "I'm assuming you're interested in one, maybe two or more of our outstanding vehicles and would require a special discount?" This, of course, is all very standard, but what I say next stuns him.

I lean back into the leather. "What I'd like to do is buy every single car you have."

For a moment, he's speechless. "I ... I beg your pardon?"

"You heard, and I'll take the garage too. In fact, I'd like to buy your entire business and I'm not going to take no for an answer."

His eyes widen and he remains in this comical pose for several seconds whilst he tries to find his voice. He must be close to retiring anyway, so surely the prospect of selling everything might not be such a bad idea to him.

He squints and shuffles uncomfortably in his seat, which will soon belong to me. "You ... you'd like to buy my showroom?"

"Mr. Astor, I *am* buying your showroom," I lean forward and slap the table, "all you have to do is name your price."

Only very rarely do people refuse to sell willingly, given the sums I offer, though occasionally some very hard bargaining is required. But I'm dealing with a seasoned car salesman here and for a moment I fear this might not be one of the easier transactions I've had to make.

We get our lawyers on a conference call and as anticipated, thirty minutes later, he's handing over the papers and a bunch of keys, and it looks like I've now added a luxury car showroom to my ever expanding portfolio of businesses.

"Well, that was quite unexpected." He blows out air. "Would you like me to introduce you to the staff, let them know that you're the boss now?"

I'm quick to jump in here and request that he simply walks out the back door without saying a word. He's a bit weirded out by this, but given the fact I've just paid the man $20 million and he's almost certainly thinking only of purchasing a villa on some Greek island, he puts up no argument and soon disappears, scratching his head.

I sink back into my new chair, prop one Italian shoe on my new table, exhale and take in my new toy. I consider strutting back into the showroom this minute and firing them all on the spot but decide it might be more enjoyable if instead, I return as my alter ego, Jimmy the homeless guy, just to see if this time they treat me any differently. It would be their final chance at redemption.

I leave via the back door and an hour later I'm returning, though this time I'm not Thor in his Ferrari, but Jimmy driving the three hundred thousand dollar car instead, just to fuck with them further.

Piers, the manager, or should I say, former manager, comes over immediately and opens the door, but does so with the most comical expression I've ever seen. Both women have also dropped what they were doing to rush over. "Sir, um, how may I help you?" His voice is several octaves higher than it was before.

I scratch at the beard and flick a piece of crust onto my new floor. "Coffee?"

He jerks. "Excuse me?"

"I'd like some coffee."

"Um, what?" He remembers our earlier exchange and now seems lost for words. If he complies then it's an admittance that he was lying before, if he doesn't then he's making a rich man unhappy.

But it's already too late for him, I only like honest people working for me, so I set off in the direction of my new office. "Follow me, all of you."

This is the part I really love, that feeling of power you get from firing those who treated you poorly and I find that there's no better feeling in this world. At least, if there is, I've yet to find it.

I sit and gesture for the three of them to occupy the Chesterfield. It's a tight squeeze and the leather squeaks when they sit.

Piers' eyes are darting about the room, he's probably wondering where all of Mr. Astor's old family photos are, not to mention why there's a homeless guy now strutting about like he owns the place. He's quick to preempt me. "Sir, um, how about that test drive you were wanting."

I lean very deliberately forwards and link my fingers. "So now you've changed your tune, huh?" I shake my head sadly. "And all it took was for me to show up in a Ferrari. Now you have time for me, right?"

"Sir..."

I hold up a hand to cut him off. Both women are on the verge of tears. I feel bad for them, they're slightly more innocent, but they still did nothing to help me before. "In case it hasn't sunk in yet, I now own your asses, which means that now, I'm your boss." I reach into the draw and pull out their pink slips. "You're all fired." Ah, that sweet satisfaction and I take a second to inhale it before looking each of them in the eye. "I just hope none of *you* ever have to suffer the tragedy of homelessness, to know how it feels to be treated like a piece of shit." I throw the papers at them. "Now get out before I have you arrested for trespassing."

They slink out the building via the back door and then I sink back into my chair, clasp my hands behind my head and exhale a beautiful breath.

But I know that within a week the urge will return and I'll need to do it all over again.

CHAPTER THREE

Angel

"I don't know why she hates me so much, all I know is that she does and she's made that absolutely clear," I blubber to Clare in the staffroom, drenching my sandwich in tears. "Everybody knows it, that I've been singled out, which is why everyday people act surprised when I return." This morning, however, had been close because I very nearly didn't bother. It had been the sight of mom perched over the budget, biting her nails that had forced the decision upon me. "I thought she was bad on my first day but she's just getting worse and worse, and there's no telling where it might lead." That was the thing. If she wants me to quit so badly, for whatever reason, and nothing's worked so far, to where must she stoop next?

"You can't quit, babe, that's exactly what she wants," Clare grabs a tissue and wipes my face, "and she'd love nothing more than to see you like this. So stop crying."

"I just don't know what to do. Why has she made it

her mission to make my life so miserable?" I sigh into my hands and not for the first time these last few days discussing my feelings with my best friend, I really do feel close to quitting. The problem is nobody else is hiring in this small town, at least not an inexperienced young girl like me and besides, my family really needs what little money I pull in. I can't risk unemployment.

After my first day, I'd purchased a new iron and spent thirty minutes making my uniform beyond perfect. It wasn't enough though because she'd managed to find problems with my mascara, loose strands of hair, perfume she said was too overpowering and apparently, even my smile isn't broad enough. Every day, new rules and regulations appear miraculously on the noticeboard and every day, I've contravened at least one of them, which means no tips for me. After two weeks, I've yet to receive any tips at all.

No, I've long since given up expecting to receive any tips. Yesterday, Clare offered to give me half of hers, and even Ben has tried giving me some of his money, but I've always waved it away. This is my problem and I will deal with it in my own way, or not.

Clearly, she wants me to quit and although I've come very close on several occasions, the larger part of me does not want to allow her to beat me. Besides, if it wasn't me being bullied by my supervisor, it would only be the next person. Or so I assumed. "Why do you think she hates me anyway?"

Clare puts a hand on my shoulder in a gesture of comfort. "Because you're the prettiest, silly. Some women are just like that, I mean, she's not exactly much of a looker, is she? She has to take out all of that bitterness the universe has thrown at her on somebody and you're the obvious candidate because, you know, you look like you."

I know I'm not the ugliest of girls but I'm certainly not so beautiful that it should merit my being treated in such a way. "But ... but what about Maria?" I ask, referring to the girl who works weekends and who's far more beautiful than I.

"Ah, you mean Maria Carrington? The answer's kinda in the name there, babe."

"What?" My mouth plunges open. "Mr. Carrington has a daughter?"

"Um, niece."

I laugh. Thank God for Clare and her ability to cheer me up when I'm down.

I quickly finish my tear-sodden sandwich because I only have five minutes before I need to be back on duty and I still have to ensure my hair is perfect, my uniform isn't scrunched after having sat down for 10 minutes and that there's no lettuce stuck between my teeth. After getting all that out of the way, I run back down to the restaurant floor. The clock says I'm a minute early, better safe than sorry, and it looks like there's a late lunchtime rush just entering.

Alma and I make brief eye contact and immediately she checks her watch. Her lips turn down because being late is one thing she can't berate me for, at least not on this occasion, but that doesn't stop her from pacing over towards me regardless.

"I need you on top form today, missy, because that man who's just walked through the door is none other than

Mark Harrison, or Mr. Harrison to you, and since I've little doubt that you have absolutely no idea who that is, let me tell you. Mark Harrison is our local member of congress, which means you'll be extra diligent when dealing with him." She begins rubbing her chin. "On second thoughts, maybe I ought to switch you with one of the better girls? Hmmm, no, Janice just went on her break. No, you'll have to do."

I think she would rather enjoy the thought of me embarrassing myself in front of such a highly esteemed diner but I will not give her that satisfaction. "I think I can handle it," I say in a way that makes her head jerk back.

"Then go!"

I rush over to the door and Harrison immediately leers at my breasts. Of course, I'm aware men do this all the time but I'm caught totally off guard by the complete lack of discretion here. "Um, good afternoon, how many in your party?"

His friends are still coming in through the door. "Twelve," he says, whilst managing a second to meet my eyes with his, "and we'll have your best available table, if you wouldn't mind."

"Yes, this way, sir," I lead the way toward the corner and I hear him grunt from close behind.

"Not a bad piece of ass, is that, maybe I'll see about putting her on my staff, if you know what I mean." Two of his friends laugh as I clench up inside.

They're all men, what looks to be a taxpayer-funded lunch with local businessmen and lobbyists, maybe even a couple other politicians. I hand them all menus and tell them I'll return to take their orders in a few minutes.

"You can cook my pork any day." The congressman says too loudly as I'm walking away. I'm cringing inside but Alma's watching me keenly so I just grin and bear it. Compared to her, a few sleazy politicians are nothing.

After a few minutes, I return and take their orders, one by one. Finally, I ask Mr. Harrison what he'd like for lunch.

He again stares at my breasts but his eyes wander further down and there's no way I'm not supposed to have noticed. "Today, I'm aching for a side of beef."

I think ... I mean ... I assume I know the distasteful innuendo he's trying to make but I play ignorance and write it down because, well, what else can I do. And it's not like our uniforms are alluring in the slightest. We look like Victorian maids.

"And for dessert, I think I'll pop a few cherries." Several of his colleagues again laugh at that, but at least there are a few who don't find the odious man funny at all.

I write it down, "thanks," and walk away biting my tongue. If it wasn't what he really wanted then he has nobody to blame but himself.

Alma's looking at me funny and she makes a *come here* gesture with her finger, exactly how a mother does to her five-year-old child. She points to my underarms. "Have you not seen yourself today, madam?"

It's at this point I notice the sweat, no doubt as a result of having to take the congressman's order, and immediately I know I've cost myself yet another day's tips. Our blouses are gray, which means the stains are very visible. "I'm sorry, I..."

"You know the rules, girl, if you cannot present yourself as per the requirement of this restaurant, then you will be put on a warning." It's not even something she needs to add to the noticeboard, on this occasion she has me for real.

"I'm sorry," I can feel the tears starting to well from behind my eyes, I tried, I really did, but nothing I do is ever good enough. It looks like she's won, this horrible woman is about to get the satisfaction of seeing me break, and I'm just about to lose it, to untie my apron and throw it to the floor when Alma's gaze moves over my shoulder. After a second, her face scrunches up into a look of utter distaste. "What the fuck has the cat dragged in?"

I'm shocked, she might be a nasty woman but never before have I heard her speak like that. I can't help but turn around and when I do, there's what appears to be a homeless man shuffling inside the most upmarket restaurant in town.

"Oh, no you don't," Alma grunts under her breath as the man draws glances from the nearest diners. A young woman covers her nose.

I actually find the situation quite amusing, not only for annoying Alma, but he probably just saved me from hastily quitting on the spot. Naturally, I already know that I'm about to be assigned to deal with the man, to eject him from the premises, and so instead I take the initiative and wander over in his direction, thinking to be extra pleasant towards the man just to get one up on my awful supervisor. It might be the only chance I'll ever get.

I bounce straight up to him and give the poor man my best smile, which I don't have to fake. "Good afternoon, sir, would that be a table for one?"

Up close, he looks a heck of a lot younger than what I'd assumed from a distance, what with his filthy hair, beard and clothing, and I can't help but think that with a little tender loving care, he'd be extremely presentable. His frame is astonishing for someone who probably lives on a diet of soup and donations. He's looking straight at me, his pupils dilate within orange irises, and for a moment he's lost his voice. There's a very prominent stench of manure, as well as something else I cannot even begin to describe, and I can only wonder what the man's story is. Someone nearby coughs.

Finally, he shakes his head and croaks, "yes, dear, table for one, if that's not a problem?" It was all in the way he said it that made me think he's almost expecting to be turfed out, but I couldn't do that.

"What? That's no problem at all, sir, you're our valued guest," I pat him reassuringly on the shoulder and instantly regret it because now my hand's sticky with something gross. "Let me show you to a table."

For some reason, he jerks in surprise and then grunts, "you're, um, too kind, miss."

I use the opportunity to take a quick glance over at Alma, whose mouth has plunged wide open. "Don't mention it, the pleasure's all mine." And it really was too. There's an empty table beside Congressman Harrison so naturally, that's where I seat the customer. Two birds with one stone. I pull out the chair. "Please, let me take your jacket." I might regret this.

He turns slowly around to stare at me and I definitely notice his eyes brighten when he takes a second good look at my face and for a moment he appears unable to move or even speak. Finally, he manages to shake himself back to awareness and with my assistance, begins to wriggle out of the stinky overcoat.

For sure, it smells worse than just about anything I've

encountered in my entire life and after placing it around the back of his seat, I can distinctly feel a residue coating my fingers, almost like I've spent the last hour stroking a dog. His brown shirt, I suspect, used to be white, and is torn in at least three spots.

Judging from his broken and split boots, and hair that doesn't look like it's been washed in months, I seriously doubt this man has the funds to pay for a meal at Carrington's, although that's not for me to judge. My job is simply to take each customer as they come.

I notice people are now staring at me, not just my colleagues but patrons as well. There's a loud cough from close by. "Smells like congress after a particularly rigorous debate on sewerage. Hey, waitress, why'd you let him in?"

I ignore the congressman and hand the customer a menu. "What would you like today, sir?" I use the exact same enthusiastic tone as I do with every other customer.

He's looking at me funny, like he can't quite believe I'm being civil to him. "What? I mean," he shakes his head, blinks, and then shakes his head again, "I mean, I'll have a coffee to begin with, and some milk, on a saucer, with a teaspoon in a mug, and also the fillet steak, cooked, with roast potatoes and asparagus, please."

Now, this just happens to be the most expensive item on the menu, and now I truly suspect he's having a joke at everyone's expense, especially mine, but I remain professional and scribble it down, and that's when I feel a hand on my ass, which causes me to jerk in surprise.

"I seem to recall asking to be seated at your best available table," Congressman Harrison's leaning back in his seat and white wine spills over the edge of his glass, "this is an important government meeting, I did not envisage having to sit beside the town tramp."

That tramp's gaze is now fixed on Harrison's hand, still clutching my cheek, but then he shoots the congressman the kind of look that could shatter glass and for a moment, I fear he's about to get up to clobber him but instead he breathes, takes a second to calm himself and glances back to me. "I'll take the steak medium-rare, my love."

Now I'm the one to blink in surprise because the customer sounded suddenly very different, like he's taken a month-long detox in thirty seconds, but I shake it off and head back to the kitchen.

Alma's mouth is hanging beautifully ajar. "Missy, have you not seen that hobo? Do you really think that creature has the means to pay for his lunch? And look, he's scaring the children." She clasps her face in her hands. "And the congressman!"

He's not scaring the children at all, if anything the poor guy's a curiosity to them. He is, however, troubling Harrison, which is fine by me. I shrug. "What do you want me to do about it?" I try not to laugh because secretly, I'm loving the discomfort it's all causing Alma, though I should probably quit while I'm ahead. "For your information, he's a friendly man who just happens to be down on his luck, and how do you know it's not his birthday or that maybe he found a $50 bill on the ground? Perhaps he just wants to treat himself. Does he not deserve to eat at Carrington's just because he's not Brad Pitt?"

"Enough." She shows teeth and steps into my personal space. I hear Clare gasp from across the kitchen. "I want you to tell him to leave, right this minute."

I step away from the awful woman. "No, I refuse to do your dirty work. If you want to turf a poor man out just for his style of dress then you can do it yourself." I jerk my jaw in the direction of the man in question and notice that he's been watching the entire altercation with interest through the serving hatch. We briefly make eye contact from across the length of the restaurant until, distracted by something, he manages to pull away.

"Angel, I'm warning you," Alma's hand wraps around my wrist and now Clare bounds over from behind the computer screen, hand covering her mouth, though she wisely doesn't say anything. This could get out of hand. Alma persists, "I don't need much of a reason to have you fired, all it would take is one word to Mr. Carrington. Is your job really worth sacrificing for the likes of a hobo?"

It's so unfair. I know there's a strict dress code for the staff but there's no such thing for the customers. Alma's just being like this because of her usual Alma reasons. My gaze finds Clare, probably because instinctively, I'm needing support from a friendly face.

"Babe, just do what she says."

I gasp at that. Maybe this isn't the right line of work for me after all. I have about one second to decide what to do.

But to my astonishment, Alma strides into the restaurant herself and although I follow sheepishly after her, I've no doubt that five minutes from now, I'm out of a job.

"I'm sorry, sir," she says as her face clenches up from the stench, "but I must ask you to leave." Everybody on Harrison's table is watching whilst he fans at his face with a napkin.

The homeless man's gaze finds me and I shrug apologetically. "I'm sorry, sir, it's all my fault, please don't be mad at Alma." I feel it my duty to make my own apology, given he was my customer.

Alma twists around looking astonished that I would defend her but turns back when the man croaks, "this is because I'm poor, isn't it?" He shakes his head sadly. "Well, I'll have you know, I've been working extra hard playing my flute on Main Street and people were generous today. I was going to eat at the shelter but thought that hey, since it's my birthday, I'd treat myself to the first steak I've had since losing my home in the fire."

It's a heartbreaking story and I feel terrible for him and angry at Alma, who has no real reason for being so mean. As usual, she just can't help herself.

"I don't care." Alma folds her arms. "Sir, I will not ask you again, will you please leave."

The man rises to his feet and looks down at Alma with deliberation from his considerable height. "Are you sure this is what you want?" He asks with no small amount of gravity, for whatever reason. Again, I'm suddenly struck by his change of apparent demeanor and gravitas.

Alma nods vigorously, her face turning red from holding her breath. "Yes!"

"Then so be it." He speaks in finality, like he's secretly passing judgment over her and everybody else here. He gives me one final, wilting gaze, and is about to leave when...

Harrison perks up suddenly and by this point, he sounds quite drunk. "Yes, leave before we have to call in a fumigation crew." I feel a slap on my ass. "Waitress, how about another bottle of the Coche Dury Meursault Les Rougeots." He squeezes and I yelp. "Did I say that right?"

I'm about to throw a glass of water over the congressman but to my amazement, the homeless man does it for me.

CHAPTER FOUR

Thor

I got him with a full jug, ice and all, and the water drips down his face, neck and ears. Several people applaud, including at least three on his table.

I tell the man seated next to him, "get him out of here," in a tone that uses all the authority that comes from being able to singlehandedly fund the congressman's political opponent at the upcoming election. On second thoughts, I think I'll do just that. Maybe I'll also call in a few favors, have gossip spread about him in the media. There has to be some dirt there somewhere, especially with a man like that; lavish parties charged to the taxpayer, insider trading, who knows? All I can say for sure is that he made the wrong enemy here.

Because nobody touches *my* girl.

Yes, *my* girl!

And she *is* my girl. I'll make damned sure of that.

But who is she?

I'm still in shock. Because it's not supposed to happen like this.

They're supposed to take one look at Jimmy and be rude, horrible, mean, call the cops, lock the doors to keep him out. They're not supposed to be warm, kind, caring, helpful...

And the hottest girl I've ever seen in my life!

More than once, I very nearly blew my cover. In fact, at one point, it almost looked like she could see through me, but I don't think she knows. But she will. I want her to know everything. Just as I must know everything about her!

No, more than that. I must have her. Own her. Possess her. Give her my babies. Many babies.

The congressman's already a blur as he's taken outside and now, I can concentrate on nothing other than the girl.

She looks sad. I think she's in trouble with the old woman, who I'm guessing is her manager. I'll fix that, whatever it is, and everything else. Because I'm minutes away from owning this place.

Shit. Usually, I'm exhilarated about making the big reveal, but now, here, at Carrington's, I'm only nervous. Really nervous. The girl, the one who's still staring at me, she's floored me.

Must get it together Jimmy, I mean Thor.

And then I remember I'm still dressed as Jimmy. Oh, that's attractive.

"Why are you still here?" It's the old woman who screeches, too close to my ear, but at least she's managed to snap me out of my trance. "That was a very esteemed diner and I voted for him." There's a surprise. She turns to my girl, my angel. "And you, Angel, in case you hadn't guessed it yet, you're fired."

Angel.

It's almost like it was meant to be.

"No!" But now she's crying and it causes me only pain. "Please, I was only..."

"Save it," the old woman smiles but quickly manages to conceal it, she hates my Angel, "I'm going to tell Mr. Carrington right now."

I've heard enough. Nobody makes my Angel sad. Like Clark Kent ripping away his suit, I throw off the wig and slowly peel away the beard. I'm still wearing a torn shirt and manure caked boots but I think I've made my point.

The manager recoils in fright, *what has she done*, whilst Angel's hand gravitates to touch her heart. People are gasping and clutching pearls all around.

I take ahold of Angel's hand, gently caressing her smooth skin with my thumb, which is all I need to do for the blood to begin surging through my manhood so that I can already feel myself growing, aching. I look her intently in the eyes and tell her, "don't go anywhere, I will fix this and that's a promise."

She nods. She trusts me. As she should.

"Oh, will you now," the woman says.

It pains me to have to avert my gaze from Angel to address the other. I growl, "you were about to see the owner, I believe, so why don't you lead the way."

She laughs. "Why not, I'm in need of a good laugh."

The chefs and other waiting staff all stare at me as I'm led through the kitchen, up some stairs, along a corridor and then she knocks on a door.

"Enter," comes a voice from behind it.

I enter first and she shuffles in after me, shaking her head. "I'm sorry about this, Mr. Carrington, the cats have been busy today."

I have no idea what she means by that but I reach forward to offer my hand to the man. "Hello, sir, my name's Thor, it's nice to meet you."

He takes my hand. It's a sickly grip. "Um, nice to meet you too." He sniffs and glances at the woman, as if expecting an explanation. "Alma? Perhaps you'd like to start."

She steps forward and coughs, regrets it and shuffles away. "Well, as you can see or, rather, smell, I asked this, um, man to leave the restaurant, only, he decided to make a scene and threw water over a particularly esteemed guest."

He shifts in his seat so that the leather makes a strange sound. "Oh, I see. Who was it?"

"Congressman Harrison."

He slaps the table. "Good. He's an odious man. What else?"

Alma gasps. I grin. This guy might be alright. I lean forward and place both my hands on his table so that I loom down on him. "Mr. Carrington, the thing is, I have a little bit of an issue with a very different incident that transpired downstairs and feel I must do everything in my power to ensure the correct outcome. That's why I'm here."

His expertly plucked eyebrows pull together. "Oh? And what is that outcome?" He glances at Alma, totally confused.

She braves the stink to step closer. "Yeah, Mr ... whoever you are, what are you going to do?"

I want to see her face for this part so I turn to her when I say it. "Mr. Carrington, I'm buying this place, so why don't you name your price."

She bursts into laughter and slaps the tabletop. "Oh, that's a good one, an out of town vagrant wants to buy the best restaurant for miles around."

I'm still looking at her when the man whose name is on all the stationery says, "wait, you're Thor Castleton."

"Huh?" Suddenly, Alma looks like she's been slapped in the face.

The owner starts rustling through a stack of magazines on the bookshelf and I already know which one he's about to pull out. "Here," he produces a copy of Men's Health magazine from sometime last year. My sister doesn't know how right she was but what can I say, I'm modest, in fact, I'm the kind of man who dresses like this even though I can afford to buy my own chain of high-end fashion stores.

Carrington flicks through the pages. "Yes, here you are, you bought out one of America's largest health club franchises." That's what happens when the manager of my local gym refuses to permit entrance to Jimmy - I buy the whole chain. He lingers on the photo and bites his bottom lip. If I recall, they made me pose in my trunks. Finally, he manages to pull himself away. "I'm sorry," his voice is suddenly very faint, "you said you want to *buy* my restaurant?"

I spare a glance for Alma, who's been very quiet this last minute. "No. I said I *am* buying your restaurant. Shall we call our lawyers?"

He sucks on his bottom lip. Glances once to Alma. Back to me. And finally, he holds out his hand. "Five million dollars?"

It's a lot more than what I would have wanted to pay for it, but that was before knowing it came with a certain little Angel. "Deal." I reach forward to grasp his hand. It's a fucking bargain!

Alma looks like she's about to be sick.

"Oh, and Alma," I say, as I take the seat opposite the former owner, "you're fired."

CHAPTER FIVE

Angel

*A*lma's been gone for a while and now everybody's talking.

After the lunchtime rush ended and the last customer had left, Janice made the decision to close the doors until further notice.

"Whatever they're discussing, it must be good," Clare says as we clean the tables. "Anyway, that homeless guy seemed to like you, don't you think?"

When he'd taken my hand, I'd definitely felt some kind of a stirring deep down in my belly. That was no ordinary homeless guy. I turn away, all shy suddenly.

She nudges me with an elbow. "Maybe he could take you back to his cardboard box," she says as she flicks some of the spilled water at me.

"Oh, stop it," I flick some back. A full jug had been thrown over Harrison. Maybe I should thank the guy, that's if he ever returns.

And just then Alma comes running through the restaurant. She's crying and there's a pink slip of paper flapping about in her hand. Everybody knows what that means and I hear at least three chefs cheering from the kitchens. Within a second the cheer spreads and then everybody's laughing, roaring and slapping tables. Alma reaches the door and attempts to exit but finds that it's locked.

"Oh," she wails, too ashamed to ask for help, and the cheer intensifies at her misfortune. Eventually, Janice takes pity and opens the door and then she's slinking outside just as a torrential downpour starts.

"That is so awesome." Clare slaps me on the back. "Looks like you won, babe."

I shift onto my other foot, the dirty table temporarily forgotten. I mean, I wasn't her greatest fan but that was pretty harsh, and I definitely wouldn't have wished her out of a job, even if that was precisely what she was about to do to me.

What is going on?

For the next hour there's no more news, which only intensifies the rumors. At one point, Karl even went up to see Mr. Carrington but he was only told to leave and he came back down shaking his head. Janice is overstaying her shift, so keen for gossip that woman is, and only later on does it occur to her that with Alma now gone, she's the one now supposedly running this ship.

And then Ben dashes into the restaurant and pants, "meeting, now, staffroom."

There's a rush to get there first but I enter last, just behind Clare. Mr. Carrington's standing beneath his portrait and beside him is a man I've never seen before in my life. He's wearing one heck of a snappy suit and spots me immediately, his eyes refusing to look away. I recognize those deep orange irises or, at least, I'm pretty sure I do, but it can't be. I'm squinting at him now but the intensity of his gaze from across the room soon has me looking down to the floor as my entire body seems to tingle.

"Who the heck is he?" Clare mutters from beside me. "Now *that* is what I call a man."

Carrington clears his throat. "I won't keep you long, my children, but there are about to be some changes made around here." He checks his watch and it's only now I notice the travel brochure clutched in his hand. He uses it to gesture to the man beside him, who's so tall and put together that he makes Mr. Carrington appear tiny by comparison. "Maldives introduce you to..." he coughs into a closed fist, "excuse me. *Might* I introduce you all to Thor Castleton, who's you're new Barbados." He mutters something to Thor that I don't hear, Thor nods, and then Carrington's removing the portrait from the wall. "Well, have fun, children, and bon voyage." He squeezes past and leaves, doesn't bother looking back. To be fair, it wasn't much of a parting speech.

I'm sure I'm not the only one who can no longer avert their eyes from Thor and I've now absolutely no doubt that this is the same man who'd been the source of all the earlier drama, his eyes, smoldering good looks, as well as instinct all tell me that this is him, the homeless guy. Yes, I'm confused right about now.

His brown hair is swept back stylishly and his trim beard gives him a look of power. His eyes hold an incredible intensity, like he's lived a life far beyond what his age might imply. He's muscular but his tailored suit, that looks like it's worth more than the average car, fits perfectly around his size and shape. But most of all, Thor has that little something else that cannot be identified, and certainly cannot be learned, because it comes from the confidence that the power I'm sure he possesses has bestowed upon him.

Again, his gaze finds a straight path through everybody else and claps onto me. "I would speak alone with Angel. The rest of you, take the night off. Go."

For a few seconds, everyone remains rooted and I can sense more than a few people are looking straight at me. Yes, there was an incident, and I was at the center of it. And now I'm sensing what's about to happen.

I'm going to be fired, just like Alma was.

"Good luck, babe," Clare says and brushes my arm as she files slowly outside with everyone else. The door closes and now I'm alone with what has to be the most devilishly attractive man I've ever seen.

And he's about to fire me.

"Angel," he moves forward and takes my hand and my body is immediately assailed by sensations I've never before known, "do not look so afraid, I can't bear to see it."

I feel so small before him, indeed, my hand is consumed by his and I have to tilt my head back to see his face. "Um," I swallow, "what happened to Alma?"

His jaw clenches briefly. "You won't ever have to worry about her ever again, your job here is safe, but if you choose it, you will never have to work another day in your life."

I'm stunned into silence by his words and I'm not completely sure I know what he means, though there's no mistaking the intention behind his gaze. "So, I'm not going to be fired?"

His eyes widen for the briefest of flickers. "Fired? God, no. You're the most wonderful waitress I've ever encountered." So it *was* him. "Do you recognize me?"

I nod. "You're the sweet homeless man, but…"

"But I'm not so sweet anymore," he finishes for me, matter of fact.

"Oh?" I hiss.

The moment's so surreal, so strange but in the most wonderful way that it almost feels like I'm floating. I'm not even sure how long I've been standing here, my hand melting into his.

"You, um, you look different," that was an understatement, and I feel so stupid for having stated the obvious.

But he just grins, confident that I've all but fully wilted before him. If he wanted he could take me right now, cast me to the couch and have whatever fun he desired with his investment, and I'd be powerless before him. But Thor Castleton is a man who can control his urges until the moment's right. "Let's go for a walk," he says, and I'm both thrilled at the thought yet disappointed that he hasn't yet picked me up with the effortlessness of which I know he's capable and done to me what I know he wants to do.

The lights are dimmed and there's an unfamiliar eerie silence as we make our way through the empty restaurant, that I guess now belongs to the man whose hand has never left mine. He grabs an umbrella and pops it open as we exit and lock the door. It's a steady rain, not as bad as when Alma left, but I'm glad to have the cover this night.

Thor places his arm around my midriff and pulls me into him, though it's not done in a way that's meant to make me believe he's doing it merely to shield me from the elements. No, he's being possessive, already demonstrating that I'm his woman.

We're heading downtown where the music is loud and people come stumbling out of the bars. I usually avoid this place, especially at this time, but I feel so safe with Thor. Ahead, on the sidewalk cramped against the walls is a line of tents, cardboard boxes or otherwise men lying on the hard ground with only a blanket for warmth. Liquor bottles lay empty or kicked over beside them, a few of the poor men have dogs, which they cuddle as though they were their only friend in the world. We come to a stop two storefronts away.

"Tell me what you see, Angel," he says my name like he's reading poetry.

Not wanting to disappoint him, I wait and watch as people walk past without so much as a care, their empty cups, there in the hope of receiving change, ignored. One man, having just left a bar, leans over a nearby trashcan and vomits. Another laughs, while someone else spits close to a sleeping man's head.

I feel suddenly very sad. "I see homeless men."

"No, Angel," his fingers pulse against my hip, "what you see is a rotten waste of human potential." He approaches the first three men and speaks words to them that I'm unable to hear. He then shakes their hands and although I'm not certain, I suspect he's discreetly handing over some dollar bills. He returns to me. "Every single one of these men once held dreams but circumstances instead conspired to put them here. This could easily happen to any one of us." It's all in the way he said it that makes me question if he once had lived like this. "Believe me, Angel, it can happen to any one of us and at any time and when that time nears, there's only one thing that can save us..." he lets go of my hip and moves around to face me. "Tell me, sweet Angel, why did you disobey your boss and risk losing your job, all for a downtrodden man you didn't even know?"

I make a deep sigh. "It was just the right thing to do."

"Yes, Angel, that's true, but you did it because of kindness. The moment I entered the restaurant, I could see it in your face." He shakes his head and lets out a deep breath. "You were meant to be like everybody else, you were supposed to be like these drunken men you see walking past now, you should have dismissed me and cast me out into the rain. But because you didn't, Angel, you have instead given me a problem."

I'm looking deep into those orange eyes as the rain begins crashing against the umbrella. "What's that?"

"Now I have to make you mine forever." He means it and I'm powerless to object, even if I wanted, which I don't. "But for the here and now, Angel, let's leave this place, let's have some fun."

He leads me away.

She is indeed as sweet and innocent as I'd imagined, a girl who I'm sure has never been touched, never been pinned to a bed beneath the weight of a man, been entered and ravished vigorously until his seed spills inside of her.

I want her first time to be special, magical, perfect, which means she must first come to love me, and I will do everything in my power to ensure that she does. Which is why I now ask her, "what is it you like to do?"

She giggles and I can tell she's thinking of some happy childhood memory. "I've always been happiest when I'm cooking."

"Ah," the pieces are beginning to fall into place, "but you work as a waitress. Why not in the kitchen?"

She squeezes my hand and I can immediately feel my cock straining against my pants. Truth is it's pretty fucking painful. "Um, well," she begins in the shy way I'm coming to expect, "there were no vacancies, only waitress positions, and Carrington's was about the only place willing to hire an eighteen-year-old without qualifications."

"So why not get your qualifications?"

She then tells me about her family situation, about her pops dying and leaving the family with a tonne of debt. She had to abandon her plans to go to culinary school in order to take the first job that came her way, just so she could help out her family, which by the way includes triplet sisters. The admiration I hold for my Angel grows by the minute. She doesn't know it yet, but all her prayers will be answered.

"So, you like to cook? It just so happens I know a place."

I want to show Angel that I'm not merely a man trying to set the world right, as Sissy puts it, but that I have a fun streak too. We return to Carrington's where the dim lights, as well as the rain smashing against the windows, provides an electrifying ambiance.

I still haven't even seen my new kitchen and when we do enter, the breath escapes me. I open out my arms, "what will it be?"

She rises on her toes and clasps her hands beneath her chin in the most adorable way imaginable. "Working here, I've had to cart around so many shrimp salads and they all look amazing. We just have to give it a try."

"Shrimp salad it is but first," I slowly, gently, and very deliberately begin loosening her blouse, one button at a time, "if we're doing this, then we're doing it properly."

She's under my control as I work, doesn't move, and as I approach the final top button, I feel her sweet breath on my hand.

I gently remove the garment, left arm, then right, and let out an almost silent hum in appreciation for how she looks in the white shirt beneath. I place the blouse over the back of a stool and grab two aprons from the hook before placing the strap of one around her neck. I feel the fullness of her breasts lightly touching my chest as I reach around from in front to tie the ends at the small of her back whilst giving her a gentle caress in that most sensitive of areas.

I hear her swallow as I step away to unbutton my suit jacket and then it enshrouds Angel's blouse when I place it on top. I put my head through the loop myself but turn around so she can tie the ends for me and even from the way she does this, I can sense how gentle she is. If I can get through this without fucking her on the countertop, it'll be a miracle and besides, it'd ruin the shrimp.

She hesitates before the large kitchen surrounding her.

I take her hands and lightly squeeze. "Don't be overwhelmed, my Angel, you can do it." I know she's nervous about disappointing me so I leave her to find her feet whilst I go to select a bottle of wine.

My new rack is extensive, maybe thousands of bottles from all over the world, but I soon find a good white from the Lombardy region of Italy. I estimate it's worth at around $200, not the most expensive in the world, but certainly perfect for tonight.

When I return, the bacon's frying, the shrimp is in the oven and she's slicing the tomatoes. She glances shyly at me from the corner of her eye and gives a little wiggle of her ass. I pour two glasses of wine whilst feasting on the sight of her curves.

"To the future," we clink glasses and take our first sip together as a couple. It won't be our last because Angel will be living the good life from now on. Her blue eyes are like oceans and they sparkle at the taste.

I take the lettuce and begin slicing.

She puckers her lips appreciatively at my skills. "Where did you learn to do that?"

I give her a playful wink, "oh, just some guy I know."

She doesn't yet know that I own my own chain of Italian restaurants, purchased after a similar dispute with a maître d'. I'd brought in my own people, which included a man by the name Valentino Rossi, who was once rated the top chef in all Emilia Romagna. He taught me a few tricks.

I take a slice of tomato and slowly tempt it before her lips. They're wide, thin and red as the fruit I now feed to her. I wait until she swallows until I move my lips close to hers and then she throws her arms around me and I'm pulling her hard into my chest as our mouths press hard together.

I can faintly taste the wine but the overwhelming sensation is the smoothness of her face against my rough. I run my hands down her body so that I can feel her soft curves and stop at that tiny midriff and squeeze. I gently feel the air pushed out from her nose and the little sigh she makes into my mouth is delightful. I'm absolutely raging down below and can think of nothing but pinning her against the work surface and pounding her like a tenderizing mallet does a fine piece of sirloin. But I won't. Not yet.

Instead, the pan fizzes, the smell of bacon is incredible, and we break apart to painfully finish the job of cooking.

She pants as she mixes the bacon into the salad and I go to remove the shrimp from the oven, the pleasant picnic image on my apron being distorted by the bulge of my own cucumber. A minute later we're seated in my new restaurant; wine, rain, candles, some classical music playing low and the most beautiful girl in the world.

CHAPTER SEVEN

Angel

*I*t's like I'm living in a fantasy world.

One moment, I was being bullied and was in fear of losing my job and the next, I'm being swept off my feet by the most ruggedly perfect man I've ever come across in my life.

The butterflies he gives me are intense, so intense that I worry I'll make a mistake, do something that might displease him or worse, that I'll wake up and this will all be a dream.

He's so dominant that if he decided to take me at any point then I'd be completely under his spell. I'd spent so long willing for him to kiss me that it was beginning to drive me crazy, but he knows exactly what he's doing, he made me wait and wait until I was screaming inside for him to do it, but when he finally did, it was like nothing I've ever experienced before.

I felt so small and helpless when he enveloped me in his arms, yet so protected at the same time. His body felt so hard through his shirt and I could feel the power pulsing from within his arms. He knows exactly how rough to be, his hands clasping around my belly, pulling me hard into his bulge, which I could distinctly feel through our aprons. I definitely felt a stirring down there, my body knows it's being seduced and I want nothing more than to give myself to him, but I also know he's going to frustrate me, to make me wait until I'm bursting to be spread out and taken.

Back to the dinner, sigh, the shrimp is delicious and he now feeds me one directly from his fork. "You look like there's something you really want to ask me." He grabs my palms from across the table. "You may ask me anything you want."

Great, now he can read my mind too, and the question I have for Thor is the obvious. "How come there's no lucky girl who's yet managed to tie you down?" I mean, he's obviously rich beyond my wildest dreams, confident, caring, and he looks like *that*.

He pushes his empty plate aside. "Angel, I am in the uniquely privileged position to have experienced both extremes of the wealth divide. I grew up in the slums of one of the largest cities in the country and for a time, even lived on the streets. Let me tell you, I know what it's like to be poor and how people treat you when you're down. Now that I'm, shall we say, in a considerably better position, only now are people willing to give me the time of day." He has me captivated as he slowly turns his wine glass. "I'll also tell you that I know what it's like to be in the middle, to be normal, to struggle with the bills, to pay the rent, to purchase a car, fighting to get ahead in this life. Well, you might be surprised to learn that when you're just like everybody else, people treat you only marginally better than when you're sleeping amongst the rats."

I find my head nodding along to his every word. This man could have any woman he wants but it sounds to me like finding that one who doesn't care about his money has been a problem.

"I could never rest easy with a woman knowing she was only with me because of my wealth, that is why I do what I do, I carry those same principles into my business and so far, it has not failed me yet." He stands and walks around the table, takes my hand and pulls me up. "You were exactly the same to me when you thought I was poor as you are right now, and that is why I will never let you go."

And at that, he scoops me up and then I'm in heaven, floating through the restaurant. He kicks the door open then another, carries me down the corridor, up the stairs while my arms clasp tightly around his neck, the staffroom's right ahead and he presses against the door with his back, carries me across the room and lays me down on the couch.

He backs away so he can discard his shirt and I'm quick to fumble with my own, my fingers shaking as they struggle with the buttons. We're both panting, my head is swirling, he throws his shirt to the floor to reveal dense muscles that twitch as he unbuckles his belt. My eyes are instinctively drawn to *that* area, and the rather prominent shape straining from within his very well-fitted pants. Finally, I cast aside my shirt and his eyes eat up my breasts from within the confines of my bra. I almost can't believe I just undressed myself in front of a man, *this* man, but it feels so right.

He kicks off his shoes and tugs his pants free to reveal

powerful thighs that soon he will use to drive himself into me. Never before have I felt so vulnerable as now, as he moves forward, looming down from above, while he fiddles with my heel straps and throws them over his shoulder. I'm apprehensive but in the most delightful way as Thor takes ahold of the turn-ups around my ankles and gives me a look as if to suggest I should be quick with the buckle. I fumble for a time bordering on being too long, but only because I can't take my eyes off his chest, abdominals, shoulders, arms but somehow I manage and then my pants are being pulled down my legs.

In the moment, I'm terribly self-conscious, *does he like me*, but his eyes absolutely feast on my legs, the curvature of my hips, my belly and a little spot still concealed beneath my underwear.

Thor lowers himself down on top of me, placing most of his considerable weight on his forearms and I waste no time reaching around his back and pulling him in tight. His lips immediately find mine, our tongues clash in hot passion, the thick musculature of his back, my legs wrap around his ass, ankles hooking together as he powerfully humps me through two very thin layers of fabric. I feel his size rubbing, pressing against my most sensitive area, all kinds of nerve endings electrifying and my passage coating with a slick substance in preparation.

He reaches around my back, unhooking my bra and I quickly release my arms for him to cast it to the floor. He seizes my breasts as the rain lashes against the windows and a moan escapes me when he covers my nipple with his mouth. I arch my back as his tongue swirls, push my hips harder against his manhood, willing him to enter me even though I know we're still encumbered by too much fabric.

He moves his kisses down my body and stops only when he reaches my underwear, tucking his thumbs inside the elastic and gently sliding it down the length of my legs. The pupils within his orange eyes enlarge and he can't resist bringing his mouth over my pearl, swirling his tongue and gently sucking. I feel a finger enter inside of me before slowly pulling out and searching back inside. It hurts but in the most delicious way and besides, I think I'm in deep need of gently breaking in.

I again hook my legs around his back and draw him closer, signaling what I'm willing for him to do to me, he's torturing me but I think he's enjoying making me burst.

"I'm going to make you mine forever," he hisses as he reaches back to work his underwear from his buttocks and down his thighs, finally releasing that swollen organ I've been dying to see, touch, taste, have inside of me.

He moves onto his knees as my gaze fixes upon his manhood and I intake an involuntary sharp breath of air as the grin slowly curls on his lips. He gently milks his considerable length, spreading what small amount of substance is already discharging from the tip to add some much needed lubrication. I'm already soaking down below, my own juices mixing with his saliva, and I hope I'm now ready to receive him, to become his, forever.

"Please, make me yours," I say as I feel my heart pounding so hard from within my chest.

He positions himself at my entrance, gently parts my lips and slowly sinks inside. He stops when my nails dig into his forearms, his width stretching me further than what's comfortable, but after a second, my body seems to adjust and the deep throbbing I feel is my body screaming that it wants more, to be filled completely.

For such a big man, he's very gentle and takes his time, only pushing as far as is comfortable for me. Several times he has to stop when my fingers dig into his biceps and then loosen as a signal to enter me further. He repositions onto his elbows so he's at a better angle to fully impale me and as he does he smothers my neck with his lips. I wrap my arms around his back and finally, he drives all the way forward, right up to the hilt. I let out a silent moan as my body adjusts to the feeling of being full, my walls clenching obscenely tight around his girth. Our eyes connect and for a moment, his gaze appears to bug out from being so tightly squeezed, almost like we're both adjusting to the feeling.

He slowly slides out and then pushes back inside, his hands covering my breasts, and he only needs about four or five strokes before I'm arching my back and clamming up with my climax, my passage pulsing around his manhood and then I'm sweating hot and cold both, my flesh tingling, breathing hard into his ear while I shake and shiver beneath him. He takes that as his signal to go and then he's increasing his speed, stroke length, as well as power, and he's smashing into me, panting and groaning, his hand clasping a fistful of hair, pounding, and then I'm climaxing for the second time and he grunts, seizes up, I feel the heat rush through his flesh as his entire body almost feels like it's going limp and rigid at the same time and then he's spilling his seed inside of me, long, hot, sticky ropes until finally, they stop and his body sags on top of mine.

"I'm inside you now forever," he sighs into my ear, "my sweet Angel."

We fall asleep in each other's arms.

CHAPTER EIGHT

Thor

My entire body seizes and clenches, forcing me to rouse from my sleep. I open my eyes and there's an angel with her mouth around my head, working my length energetically with her little hands just as I explode into her mouth.

"Fu....." my hair's damp and I brush my hands through it as she works every last drop of my seed out from my balls.

I must be one heck of a deep sleeper but it's sure a nice way to wake up.

"I think I'm going to enjoy knowing you," I pant and gesture for her to join me back up the couch. She does, licking her lips. We're both still fully naked from last night and I envelop her nakedness in my arms. "Today, we will have some fun but later on, I have a surprise for you."

Her face brightens in the most adorable way. "Oh, what is it?"

I shake my head. "No, it's a surprise."

"No, please tell me," she grabs ahold of my arm and gives it a shake, "I hate surprises."

I laugh, she amuses me without even having to try and I think I will enjoy keeping it from her for a while, even after that good morning she just gave me.

We use the staff facilities, showering together, and of course, I take the opportunity to pin her front-facing against the wall so that I can drive deep into her pussy from behind, smashing her cheeks hard while the hot water cascades down upon us. I don't think I'll ever get bored of Angel.

Luckily, she has a change of clothes in her locker, and I'm fine in the simple jeans and t-shirt I always carry around in my bag. When she arrives back from the changing room wearing her civvies, cut-off denim shorts and a red tube top, I'm even more awestruck by her beauty than ever.

I whistle, "looks like we'll have to think about changing the uniform at this place."

She gives me a shy little twirl, my eyes not once leaving her ass. "Ready when you are, mister."

I put my arm around her waist as we walk down the stairs and emerge in the restaurant. There are people working down there, rearranging tables, hanging new curtains, placing up new portraits, painting the walls and there's one of my managers conducting an induction with what looks like a group of new staff members. Of course, my sister's there with a cell clamped against her ear as she directs traffic. She sees me immediately, does not miss the hot girl I'm with, and ends the call.

Angel's fingers pulse around my side and that she looks up at me with alarm does not escape my attention.

"Sissy," I say as she approaches, "you weren't instructed to begin here. At least not yet."

She flaps a dismissive hand, not once taking her eyes off Angel. "Hello, I'm Thor's sister, Mellisa," she looks uncomfortable and then I see why.

Her friend Kristina's lurking just behind her, she has hippie braids now and is actually holding what has to be a crystal. She throws it to the tiles and runs out the restaurant.

"Oh, gosh," Angel sighs, "what happened?"

"My friend was hoping to date my brother, is what happened," Sissy spoke petulantly to my Angel and I don't like it one bit.

I feel Angel's hand wilt from my side. "Sissy, how many times must we have this conversation, Kristina will have to get over it." I pull Angel into my side. "As you can see, I'm with Angel now, so you'd all better get used to the idea because she's not going anywhere and neither am I."

Her hand returns to my side.

My sister notices this. "My brother doesn't like giving people second chances, which is something you should know about him, just in case, you know, you should ever happen to make the slightest error over the smallest thing."

I feel my blood pressure rising and remember that Sissy didn't answer my earlier point. "Why are you here? I didn't instruct you to come yet."

She shrugs, "I'm your organizer, duuurr." That's right, of course. Sissy always whips my new businesses into shape, which usually entails interior designing, new branding, publicity and of course, firing and hiring new staff."

I check my watch. The people who were here yesterday, Angel's friends, they haven't arrived yet, and there's a group of new people sat at the large table being inducted. Shit.

And it looks like Angel's realized it too. "Thor, why isn't Clare here, and Ben and Janice, and all the rest."

I have to breathe to keep from shouting at my little sis, what has she done? Worse, she's made Angel sad.

"Oh, don't you know," Sissy begins, "he always cleans out the old people, which is why I'm kind of surprised you're still here."

I've heard enough, I grab Sissy by the wrist and pull her into the kitchen. She comes willingly enough.

I exhale deeply and pinch at the skin atop my nose. "Ok, what's the matter?"

"Isn't it obvious?" She folds her arms and begins tapping her foot. "I told Kristina I'd do my best to set the two of you up and here you are coming down the steps with some..."

"Don't say it!" I interject with a warning hand. I've had just about enough of this. "Listen and listen carefully because this is the last time I'm going to tell you. I will never date your friend, so you will *both* have to get over it."

She pouts, she might be a strong woman but a telling off from big brother soon makes her look like a child again. "I ... you know I just want to see you happy and settled. I'm ... I'm so proud of you but there's a big piece that's missing and..."

"And now I have it with Angel." I allow my face to soften, I probably won't fire her over this, which would be the last thing I'd ever want to do because... "and you're wrong Sis..."

"Wrong? About what?"

"If I didn't give people second chances, you'd be long gone by now."

She punches me on the shoulder. Looks like things are back to how they ought to be.

"I want you to hire the old staff back, all except for that Alma woman."

She nods. "Anything else?"

"Yes. Is that surprise still good for later?"

She laughs, "oh, yes, of course. She must be very special if you're going to this much trouble for her."

I give my Sissy a hug and say, "she is, now let's go back and meet her properly."

Because it's time my woman and I went out to have some fun.

CHAPTER NINE

Angel

We're in the back of Thor's chauffeur-driven limousine, the dividing wall's up and we're heading to... well, he hasn't told me where we're going and every time I try to ask, he just pulls me in for a kiss and it always turns into something longer and by the time we're done I've forgotten what I was meant to be asking. He knows how to frustrate me, but in the best possible way.

When we're not kissing, we're talking. Talking about everything. I learn that Thor's a keen golfer and owns his own course somewhere out west. He's traveled all over the world, though only more recently when he began taking a more hands-off approach to many of his businesses. He tells me his favorite country is Italy, a place I've always dreamed of going but always knew I never would.

"Italian food was the reason I wanted to become a chef," I tell him and he links his fingers together like some evil genius. "What?" I ask. "What did I say?" I shake his arm and he starts laughing, so I shake harder and beg that he tells me what evil he's planning.

He sighs, "ok, let me tell you ... the thing is..." instead, he pulls me closer and then our lips are clashing, our tongues are dancing and his hand completely consumes my breast. By the time he's done, the bulge in his pants is obscene and I've forgotten what I was saying.

The car stops and when Thor opens the door and takes my hand to help me out, I'm amazed to find we're at the famous Laurent's. I gasp because it's only the most upmarket shopping mall in the entire state.

"Thor?"

He shakes off my objection and pulls me in the direction of the swanky building. "You're *my* girl now, and this is how my girl gets treated."

I find myself turning into him as my mouth falls silently open and my eyes begin to sparkle. "Say it again!"

He picks me up, gives me a spin and when he puts me down his hands are on my shoulders as he gazes directly into my eyes. "Angel, you are *my* girl and my girl gets treated like a queen." He opens the door to the mall and my eyes are immediately taken by all the bright lights and designer stores I've heard so much about but knew I'd never possess the funds to even consider making a purchase. "Besides," he continues, "the way you won my sister over is deserving of a reward."

I laugh and recall the memory. At the second attempt, she'd been much nicer, almost like a different person, in fact. Whatever Thor had said, it had worked.

"And why is that?" I ask.

Thor grunts, "because she's an ice woman, usually, the way we grew up, she kind of had to be. We both did, just minus the woman part for me." I giggle and he continues.

"But it looks like you've melted her the way you melted me."

I'm almost giddy when he pulls me in the direction of a shop selling designer dresses. It's not necessary at all, I'd be happy merely taking a walk in the park with Thor, but if my wearing a nice dress will make him happy then of course, I'll oblige for him. But there's one other concern on my mind and so I find myself tugging at his hand. "Oh, hey?"

"What is it, my Angel?"

I'm still shaking his arm. "You have to promise you're not going to buy any businesses and put someone out of a job today."

He tips his head back to laugh. "Just so long as they treat you the way you deserve then there'll be no problems."

Together, we approach the sales lady and instinctively, she checks out the clothes we're both wearing, Thor in simple jeans and t-shirt and me in, well, my usual attire, and I pray that she's not questioning whether we have the bankroll to be in a place like this. I suspect that nothing bad was meant by it, that it was an automatic reaction, like how hairdressers immediately glance at your hair when you walk into a salon, but I'm nervous all the same. I don't suppose she saw us get out of a chauffeur-driven limo.

She nods at Thor, "Hello, how may I..."

"Please be nice to us!" I blurt out and immediately cover my mouth.

She smiles and gives me a sympathetic tilt of the head. "I'm nice to all our customers, so you have nothing to worry about there."

Thor doubles over in hysterics and my skin turns red.

When he straightens, he finally notices the size of the store and his eyes widen. He takes the lady aside and I hear him say, "help find my girl the nicest dress in the store and I'll be back soon." He hands the lady a bank card and turns back to me. "There's something I've got to do but take your time and have fun." And with that, he walks out, leaving me with the saleslady.

I grin shyly, "typical man," and I stare after that ass with a longing.

I try on numerous dresses but I'm a girl with simple tastes, which is why we settle on an all-red halter that clings to my curves and makes my ass and breasts look delectable. The lady, who'd introduced herself as Lacy, was careful never to show me the price tag.

"You can wear it to go, if you wish?"

I agree, and Thor's strolling back in the store just as I'm leaving the fitting room. From the other side of the store, he stops, his eyes widen and his jaw drops.

I step over to him and give a little twirl. "You like it?"

He swallows and without taking his eyes off me, he says to the woman, "I'll take it ... I mean, she'll take it."

We walk out hand in hand and I say, "I know what you're thinking and I bet now you're regretting being so far from home, right?"

The look he gives me in that moment is priceless. "Yeah, just keep tempting me, my Angel, but I want you to know this, we'll be back at my home eventually and as soon as we are," he leans close so he can groan the words into my ear, "I'm gonna fuck you senseless all night long."

I sigh, I really shouldn't tease him because in the end, I'm only frustrating myself.

Thor takes me to a restaurant on the top floor and the

place is so cozy, intimate and exclusive that there are only five tables in the whole place. We order cocktails and drink from each other's straws and the food arrives in tiny, little portions in such amazing colors and it all tastes so exquisite, all nine courses. We can barely take our eyes off each other and it's now I know that I never want to be with another man for as long as I live. Thor is perfect in every way.

When we leave, I'm feeling a little tipsy and when I'm like this I tend to get mischievous. It's all in the way I'm walking so that my breasts crush against his arm. When I stop to check out a store window, it's all in how I bend forwards in full view of his gaze. And I admit that, whoops, once or twice I might have accidentally, sort of, kind of, accidentally grazed his...

"So I was right," he growls, "that second time was no accident," he scans left, right and behind, and I suspect he's searching frantically for a janitor's closet. Looks like he's fresh out of luck. "I'm warning you, my Angel, I will have you home eventually."

"What?" I give him my best look of innocence. "I have no idea what you're talking about."

"Right," he bites his bottom lip, "you know, I've an old riding crop I might need to put to good use."

He buys me a new pair of heels, an excursion that lasts about three minutes, and then we're in a leather goods store where he insists on buying me a new bag. Each time, I tell him it's unnecessary but he always perseveres.

We're leaving and walking back to the car at a clip. He tells the driver to take us back to Carrington's and then we're alone again on the back seat with the dividing wall concealing us. I half expect him to take me here and now, and I'm willing him to do so, but he's in full control of his lust and even when I stroke him through the denim of his jeans, he still manages to hold off. Though it's a close call.

"Just you wait," he pants.

It's early evening when we arrive back in town and having just got off the phone to his sister, he tells the driver to stop about a mile from our destination so that we might enjoy a walk alone. He tips his driver and we exit.

As soon as I'm out the car, I throw my arms around his shoulders. "I just want you to know that I've had the most wonderful day of my entire life."

"I'm glad," he grins, "I've had the most wonderful day too," and then we're sinking into a deep kiss as small groups of mid-evening couples, well-dressed and in love, pass us by on all sides.

It's a beautiful late fall evening, chill but not cold, at least not yet, but the weather's about to turn. I'm still hot from the ride, clutching the whole way to my man, but I'm glad it's only a short walk to the restaurant and warmth. We pass the bars and clubs, loud with music and vexing with students getting thrown out for being drunk. One of them is undoing his zipper to pee against a wall and the liquid trickles down the street to collect where the ground levels out, right where there's a group of homeless sitting before their small polystyrene cups begging for change.

When we approach, Thor does his usual thing, squeezing their shoulders, shaking their hands while, I suspect, discreetly handing over dollar bills, or saying words of love and encouragement. "If you're ever cold, please come to Carrington's. There's always a meal there waiting for you."

I know he wishes he could do more. Thor was lucky, he

got out, but not everyone has his grit, determination and resolve. But he's right, it's an awful waste of human potential. He shakes another homeless man's hand, pats his dog, and moves onto the next, a woman who's sobbing her eyes out, I guess because maybe she's newly down on her luck.

Thor crouches down, "hey there," and when Alma looks up, he staggers back.

CHAPTER TEN

Thor

One moment, I was the happiest man alive, not a care in the world, and the next there's something painful twisting in my heart.

Finally, it struck me, out here on the street, that throughout my time crusading for my cause, I'd taught a few lessons, made a few points and supposedly put the world to rights whilst making a fucking fortune in the process. But it had never dawned on me that while I was putting people out of work for being cruel to the homeless, that I myself was making more homeless people in the process.

It wasn't supposed to be like this.

"Alma?" Angel hisses whilst giving me a look that hurt. I didn't want my Angel to feel any guilt for what I'd done.

Alma, recognizing her former subordinate, yanks a blanket over her head. It was shame Alma was feeling right now. I too was feeling that.

"Alma, what happened?" Angel asks, but we all know it's obvious what happened.

There's a sniff from beneath the filthy blanket. "Go away, I don't want to be seen like this."

Angel is shaking her by the shoulder. "Alma, we already saw you, please talk to me."

After a few seconds, Alma slowly removes the blanket from her head, but she's still unable to look directly into the eyes of the girl she used to bully, the girl she used to steal from. "Well, you've seen me now, so have your laugh at my expense and leave." Her face is red and puffy, like she's had a rough twenty-four hours.

"Alma," I say crouching down again, "my Angel would never laugh at the misfortune of others." I know that to be true.

I'm joined up close by Angel. "Alma, why were you always so mean to me?"

She splutters tears. "Because I'm a bad person, which is why I deserved to lose my job and home. You did the right thing by firing me, Mister Thor." Well, if nothing else, she was certainly contrite. "I'm sorry, Angel, you deserve better than to be bullied by me."

Angel stands and pulls me aside. "Thor, my love," she presses against me and I know what's coming, she is my Angel, after all, "is there anything we can do for her?"

I take a breath and can only gaze into that beautiful, loving face. "You're the one who will have to work with her. If you think she's changed, or can change then..." besides, I still have a surprise waiting for Angel, something my sister is seeing to right this minute, and it potentially changes things.

She kisses me softly on the cheek and returns to Alma. "Why don't you come back tomorrow morning and we'll have a chat," she takes something out of her bag and goes to shake Alma's hand, "until then…"

Alma, taking what I assume to be some money for a hotel, begins balling her eyes out and embraces my Angel in a hug.

When we're out of earshot, Angel stops and throws her arms around my neck, pulls me in for a kiss and then we're breathing heavy as our tongues slide across each other and my cock strains to get out. She finally pulls away and sighs into my ear, "I can't wait to see your home."

Walking then became difficult. But I think I'm going to be very happy tonight.

We arrive back at Carrington's where my sister and a few designers are finishing up with the new floor plan.

"Wow," Angel gazes around at the walls with their new coats of paint, hangings and furnishings, "this might take some getting used to."

Sissy and I share a glance from across the floor. It looks like she's done that thing I requested of her, all the things, in fact, but one thing in particular.

"Angel," I say as I grab her hand and pull her towards the kitchen, "come with me."

"Oh, what now, oh…" she's remembered there was supposed to be a surprise and her entire body suddenly turns rigid with a mixture of excitement and trepidation, "what is it?"

"You're about to find out."

There's a man with his back turned to us and he's leaning over a bunch of recipes. He wears an all-white uniform and a chef's hat. He turns around suddenly, "ciao," he says, clapping his hands, "you must be Angel." The way he says it makes it obvious he's not from downtown but some whole other country, Italy, perhaps.

"Angel," I gesture to our newest member of staff, "I'd like you to meet Valentino Rossi," the mention of his name triggers a memory in her head from our earlier conversation. "You're going to be spending the next year working as his subordinate and he's agreed to teach you everything he knows." And after that, if she wants, she'll be Carrington's head chef.

In typical Angel style, she's shy and nervous to be face to face with one of the world's greatest chefs and only just manages to reach forward to shake his hand, her eyes barely able to meet his. "Pleased to meet you, signore."

"Please, call me Val," he beams a great wide smile and his enthusiasm is infectious. It won't take Angel long to become comfortable with him. He's a little man with a fat belly, exactly how all great chefs are supposed to be and I'm thrilled he agreed to move across state to work at one of my other restaurants.

I leave my two chefs to get acquainted while I pull my sister aside. "Thanks for organizing everything. Did you and Valentino pack our hamper?"

She nods and wipes her forehead. "Never a dull moment working for you, Thor. What'll be your next big purchase? Maybe a football team or a theme park? An airport, perhaps? There's potentially thousands of staff just waiting to piss off our old friend Jimmy."

I shake my head. "I think I'm going to have a long hard think about my future business model. Who knows, maybe I'll decide to start my own place from scratch." After all, I really miss those days, and there's so much more satisfaction in doing it yourself.

I wait just long enough to watch her jaw drop before grabbing the hamper and heading with Angel to the car.

CHAPTER ELEVEN

Angel

*W*e're taking the Ferrari, which he just happened to have parked in a nearby garage, into the western suburbs. I've never seen so many large houses surrounded by gates and all enveloped in golf course after golf course. Thor casually remarked that he'll soon teach me to play.

About half an hour out of town, he presses a button on the dashboard and then a large set of steel gates are opening out to reveal what can only be described as a modern castle.

"Thor?" I gasp, "is this where you live?"

He looks so hot in his sunglasses. "This is where I live when I'm in this state," he says as if it's nothing.

It's about the size of a small shopping mall and has fountains, a hedge maze, pond with ducks and a helipad. I dare not ask where the helicopter is because surely, he doesn't have his own helicopter. Surely!

What has to be a valet leaves the house and then waits patiently for our arrival and when Thor pulls up, we just get out and the valet jumps in and drives the car off around the back, supposedly to park the thing.

Thor's beaming, "come, let's eat," he actually says, like he owns the place, it's all still too much to believe. He carries the hamper, which is filled with items from Carrington's new menu à la my new best friend Valentino Rossi and I can't wait to dive in. "I just have to show you this place first." He pulls me into a games room that has a billiards table, darts board and a Dance Dance Revolution arcade machine.

My face brightens. "Oh, I'm so going to whip your sweet ass at this."

He puts his arm around me possessively. "We'll soon see about that."

I want to see the whole house and everything that's in it but the truth is, we're both absolutely ravenous and Thor's been seething all day whilst I've been wearing this dress. It's too cruel for either of us to wait any longer, which is why we're picking up speed as we climb the stairs, stride past a gym, private home cinema, bowling alley and art studio until finally he pushes open the door to his bedroom, which is not really a bedroom at all, but more like an entire open plan suite with living room, kitchen and everything else. The bed is just another part of the furniture.

He opens out his arms to encompass the large space. "Make yourself at home." He goes to fix up some plates and put on some music whilst I gaze at the high ceiling, tasteful decor and little bits of Thor. There are many photos with his sister and lots of tastefully uniformed staff from all kinds of businesses around the entire country. There's a map of the USA with little pins inserted where, presumably, Thor has interests. They're scattered all over the place with large clusters in certain big cities. There are also pins in Italy, France and other countries.

I walk across to the table where he's just setting down the plates. The candle's already lit and the wine has been poured. I delve into the hamper and pull out the food. Grilled octopus in a spicy vegetable sauce for starters, followed by lobster ravioli and finally a pan-seared venison medallion with a red wine sauce. It all looks beyond delicious and I can't wait to learn how to make all this stuff myself.

The wine again has the effect of making me mischievous and I wait for strategic moments, when he just happens to be watching, before innocently leaning forwards to expose my cleavage. He always goes silent when I do this and it's always followed by a sip of wine to moisten his throat.

He coughs into a fist. "You enjoying the ravioli?"

"Um-hmm," I lean casually forwards to pick up the sauce, "so delicious."

He takes a sip of wine and then another, and now he's looking at me in a way that makes me question if he knows I'm doing it deliberately.

I pour the sauce innocently over my ravioli. Sometimes torture can be fun.

I'm completely stuffed by the time it comes to dessert, crème brûlée, which is one of my absolute favorites.

Thor pulls his chair closer and dips his spoon into the dessert before holding it out for me. I lean forwards and open my mouth and somehow, he manages to get some on my chin. "Whoops, here let me get that." He kisses it off my face and then brings forth the spoon again, only this time he smushes it across my neck. "Damn it, I'm so clumsy." He moves down and covers my neck with his mouth, tonguing the sweetness from my flesh whilst seizing a breast and gently squeezing through my dress. "I know exactly what you've been doing, my Angel, but now the time has finally come. You've kept me waiting all day but now I have you all to myself and I'm about to have my way with you."

I'm already heaving with anticipation and he scoops me up and places me on the countertop before lifting the dress over my head and casting it to the nearby couch. My bra soon follows and then he's pasting the creamy goodness all over my breasts before spending considerable time cleaning it off the best way he knows how.

I'm kicking off my underwear and then smearing myself down there too. He takes his cue and pulls me to the edge for a better angle, crouches, and I find myself falling back against the plates as his tongue swirls and curls and flicks inside of me. My ankles hook behind his back, pulling him tighter and I can already feel something huge brewing from the very pits of my belly. I'm just about to explode when Thor pulls away, leaving me gasping and frustrated, but he's lifting me up again and effortlessly carrying me across the room and dumping me on the bed.

"Turn around," he grunts, and I do, hearing the zipper followed by the sound of friction as he tugs off his jeans. His thick round head teases my opening and I find myself moving back onto him, impaling myself, and then his hands are grasping hard my buttocks and then I'm being pounded, again and again, deep, powerful thrusts, stretching my passage to the limit, the sweet sound of his thighs smacking my ass, I bite into a mouthful of sheets to save from screaming, and then I'm exploding as I feel jet after jet of Thor's hot, sticky seed coating my insides. He remains in situ, his fingers rigidly digging into my flesh until he's released every last drop, and only then does he pull out so that he can carry me into his shower.

I barely even notice the gold basin and diamond encrusted cups, but within a few seconds, the water's raining down on us, my back's pinned against the wall and my legs wrap around his back as he uses the strength in his arms to hold me up. His thrusts are slow but powerful and this angle is so incredibly tight for us both that he needs only a couple of minutes before again, he's firing jets of cream deep inside of me.

Still dripping with water, we're rushing back to the bed where he pulls me on top so that I'm straddling him. I love this new angle, which means I have full control over his penetration and I can aim right for that very spot that makes my belly begin to swirl with the makings of something huge. I lean forwards, placing my hands on his hard abdominals and continue rocking as his size stretches me like never before. He's biting his bottom lip, clutching hard my hips and then his entire body bucks as he releases yet more seed to coat my passage. My body goes into rapture as I let out a scream and my muscles contract to pull Thor's nectar even further inside of me. For a whole minute, we both remain in position, shivering, shaking, sweating, our bodies slowly cooling until finally, I collapse on top of him.

I don't know for how long we both remain silent, embracing each other, but eventually Thor brings me to arm's length and delves into the pocket of his jeans, pulling out a small box.

I think I know what it might be but I still can't believe it. "Thor?" I find myself shrieking.

He opens the box, I think I recall him leaving me for a few moments back at the mall, and inside is the largest ring I've ever seen. "My angel," he begins, "you make me the happiest man in the world and it's only going to get better for us," he takes the ring out of the box and places it straight on my finger, "I knew the moment I saw you that you would be mine forever and now I'm making it official." He didn't ask and truth is he doesn't need to.

"Yes, yes, yes," I scream, "I never want to be with anyone else."

We embrace and share a long, hard, passionate kiss. He's already growing down below, and I clench my inadequate fingers around it and begin working him.

"Forever," he moves on top and I lie back and prepare to be entered.

Thor

*E*ight weeks.

That's all I needed before I took my Angel up the aisle and we were hitched.

She was already pregnant, as was my intention, and in a few short months from now, Angel will be giving birth to the first of our many children.

I stare at that ass as I approach her, leaning over the balcony, the gently rippling waves of the Mediterranean splashing against the yacht's hull not far below. She's gazing through a pair of binoculars at the Italian landmass when I press myself against her and place my hands on her belly that's carrying our child.

She twists her head to kiss me hard on the lips. "What city is that?"

"I told the captain to take us to the Amalfi Coast, so you're actually looking at a series of small towns." My cock is already swelling against her ass, it never takes much, the slightest touch of her flesh, her smell, a glance at her curves. That will never change. "Not long now and we'll berth at the harbor." And just as soon as we arrive at my villa, for the first time, I'll get to ravish her on the European continent. It won't be the last.

My Italian villa sits high on a hill overlooking the town of Amalfi, which is where they make a famous liquor from lemons. It's sweet and has become synonymous with the town. I want to show Angel everything. Experience all that the world has to offer. With her.

Two months of relaxation for our honeymoon, just me and the most beautiful girl in the world. I also have much thinking ahead of me, to decide what to do next. Just sitting back and collecting the money has never been my thing. I have to do something good with my time, my resources, my abilities and hopefully, whilst I'm here, I'll be able to figure all that out.

After two weeks, Angel's family will be joining us. I love them each already; Carol and the triplets, Kelly, Holly and Tilly, even if I can't tell any of them apart and it gets more and more embarrassing every time I say the wrong name. I tell you, I might have to start insisting they wear name tags.

Of course, I'm taking care of them too, not that Angel even asked but I insisted. They're family, after all, and I take care of what's mine. I never had much family, just me and Sissy, so seeing it expand so greatly is a blessing and I intend to make the most of it. Those three girls will go to the best colleges in the country and receive the best opportunities, and Angel's mother, Carol, will never have to work another day in her life.

We're going to be exploring Italy as a family, and we're all going to have the time of our lives.

My cell rings and I move away from Angel to answer, adjusting my trunks as I do. "Yeah?"

"Thor," it's Malcolm, one of my lawyers back home, *"looks like we did it."*

I can't keep the smile from my lips. "By how many votes?"

"Not even close. Looks like Harrison might have to get a job waiting at one of your restaurants."

"If he's lucky."

"Look, Thor, I won't keep you any longer. Enjoy your honeymoon. And congratulations!"

I end the call and gaze at the approaching town of Amalfi.

Nobody insults my girl.

Nobody.

Angel

"*B*ig order, babe, looks like a tableful of shrimp addicts, and some of them are large," Clare strings the word out and I can only gulp, hoping we have enough shrimp to go around. She passes me the order and I exhale a deep breath.

"Oh, gosh, talk about being back in the thick of it." Indeed, it's my first shift back after my maternity leave, but at least I have Valentino, well, for one more day. "Thanks again for holding the ship for me. Do you really think I'm ready?"

He throws a heap of prawns into the pan and tosses in the herbs, cream, pesto and butter. "Angel," I always love the way he pronounces my name with a hard g, "you are amazing chef and will be fine without little old me."

Still, he taught me everything I know and it will be hard to see him leave. But when you're one of the world's best chefs then I guess it's cruel to confine their talents to just one restaurant in some obscure town. That gift needs sharing. Oh yeah, Valentino isn't the only person we'll be losing.

"Are those lasagnes ready?" Alma enters the kitchen and slinks up behind the Italian before shamelessly brushing against his ass.

He spins around holding his spatula and slaps her on the leg, "ah, my favorite dish."

"Bleugghhh," I have to look away, those two never cease. Aye, it's amazing what the love of a good man can do for a woman.

My husband texts. *"Everything still all good for tonight?"*

I respond, *"You bet! And don't be late."*

He wouldn't want to miss tonight's surprise party for the world, which is why he's making extra sure there have been no last minute changes of plan. He has to travel over from the homeless shelter he built, where he's putting in a late shift teaching a business class to the residents.

I still remember the day he came up with the idea and ran jumping into the pool all excited to tell me, half drunk on a bottle of Limoncello he'd purchased earlier in Amalfi.

"I have it! I finally have it, my Angel!" He splashed water all over the place.

"Ok, but careful, my unborn child would like to have a father."

He waved it away. "I will build a homeless shelter and teach new skills, offer grants for businesses so that never again will they have to spend another night sleeping on the concrete."

I was about to tell him that it was a fantastic idea, but he was already jumping out the pool, getting on his cell and making calls. I love my husband and can't wait to have more of his children.

The last diners leave, Janice locks the doors and all everybody has to do now is clean up. I take a breath in the kitchen, happy I got through my first day back but feeling the trepidation at the thought that from tomorrow, I will officially be the head chef at this place. Wow!

Alma places down her cleaning cloth and makes her way over. For a few seconds, she just stares at me, her lips quivering in that way people do when they're about to start crying.

"Oh, no, Alma, please don't, you'll set me off too."

"Thank you again, Angel."

"What for?"

She shakes her head. "You know exactly why."

I flap a hand. "Ancient history, my sweet, and besides, if it hadn't been for all that business, I would never have met my Thor, which means you'd never have met Val either." It can be a funny old world sometimes.

"Even so…" she begins and stops. There's nothing else that needs to be said. Valentino wants to move back home and Alma's going with him. Something about a nice house he has somewhere in Tuscany, and Thor and I have been invited to visit anytime we like.

I take off my hat and embrace my old foe. I then have to keep her distracted for a few more minutes whilst everything in the restaurant moves into position. I'm watching through the serving hatch and waiting for Clare to give the signal.

"You could visit us in Amalfi too. It's where they make limoncello. You ever heard of it?" I crane my neck but Clare's only showing me her palm in a signal to wait.

Alma gives me a funny look. "We serve it in the

restaurant and ... you brought me a bottle back from your honeymoon."

"Oh," I scratch my head, "yes, that's right, um, did you enjoy it?" Still the palm.

"It made me sick," she's squinting at me now, "don't you remember? You were there."

"Ah, yes, now I remember." Hurry up! I can just make out Thor and Harry in his baby carrier, lots of movement. "So, um, what do you plan to do when you arrive in..." Clare gives me the thumbs up, "Ok, that's goodbye, Alma, have a safe flight." I'm gently shimmying her towards the restaurant and give her a gentle shove through the door.

"Surprise!!!" Everybody's here, the brass band starts up and the poppers start flying.

"Oh, my God!" Alma shrieks but quickly realizes what's happened, turns around and gives me a look I'll always remember. She's quickly surrounded by friends and colleagues all thrusting cards in her direction and there's Val with the champagne filling glasses. I step away from the madness and Thor joins me in the corner.

"A happy ending, my Angel," he looks so adorable with our beautiful baby, in fact, he's kind of making me want to start work on baby number two. He catches me looking at him. "Don't worry, I'm on it," he says, knowing full well what I'm thinking. He leans close and groans into my ear. "Nine months, maybe from this very day, and we'll have our next child."

I think he means it.

ALSO BY MAGGIE TWAIN

Pretty Nerd

Breaking Character

Saved by the Convict

Saved by the Cage Fighter

Unleashed: A Royal Romance: An English Prince At College